NORMAN BRIDWELL

Clifford's®
First School Day

SCHOLASTIC INC.

New York   Toronto   London   Auckland   Sydney   Mexico City   New Delhi   Hong Kong

For Deidre Kathleen

The author thanks Manny Campana
for his contribution to this book.

ISBN 0-439-08284-6
Copyright © 1999 by Norman Bridwell.
All rights reserved. Published by Scholastic Inc.
SCHOLASTIC, CARTWHEEL BOOKS and associated logos are trademarks and/or registered trademarks of Scholastic Inc.
CLIFFORD, CLIFFORD THE BIG RED DOG, CLIFFORD THE SMALL RED PUPPY
and associated logos are trademarks and/or registered trademarks of Norman Bridwell.

10 9 8 7 6 5 4 3 2   9/9 0/0 01 02 03 04

Printed in the U.S.A.
First printing, August 1999

I'm Emily Elizabeth. Every day I ride to school
on my dog Clifford. Clifford is too big to go inside.

Clifford hasn't been inside a school since he was a tiny puppy.

I took him one day for show-and-tell.

All the kids wanted to pet my very tiny puppy.
Miss Pearson liked him, too, but she said it was time
to begin our day.

First she put out the finger paint. I love finger painting.

Clifford got right up on the table.

He sniffed the yellow paint.

Oh my. The jar tipped over!

Clifford found out that paint is very slippery.

Miss Pearson said Clifford was a good artist.

He made a beautiful yellow picture.

We couldn't leave Clifford all covered with paint.
Miss Pearson thought that some water play might be
a good way to get him clean.

Tim had made a boat out of a milk carton.
Clifford was a perfect captain for the boat.

Captain Clifford climbed the mast
to look around . . . .

And that's how we got the paint off.

Miss Pearson dried him off. She said we were going to make cookies next and Clifford could watch. That would keep him out of trouble.

While Miss Pearson rolled out the cookie dough,
Clifford got curious about the bag of flour.

Clifford made another mess.

Miss Pearson said it might be a good idea for Clifford
to play outside. We all went out to the playground.

I thought Clifford would enjoy the slide.

He wiggled out of my hands . . .

. . . and went down the slide by himself.

He landed in the sandbox.

We helped the kids rebuild their sand castle.

We made Clifford the king of the castle.
He loved that.

Then it was lunchtime.

I shared my sandwich and dessert with Clifford.

He gobbled up his sandwich.

But he didn't know how to eat the dessert.

Poor Clifford chased the wiggly cubes all over the floor.
The other kids thought that was funny.

Miss Pearson said it was time for Clifford to go home
and have a real lunch. She told me to bring him back
to school when he was a little bigger.

She should see him now.